Sherry Garland

Children
OF THE
Dragon
Selected Tales from Vietnam

WITH ILLUSTRATIONS BY

Trina Schart Hyman

HARCOURT, INC. • San Diego New York London

www.harcourt.com

Library of Congress Cataloging-in-Publication Data
Garland, Sherry.
Children of the dragon: selected tales from Vietnam/by Sherry Garland; illustrated by Trina Schart Hyman.
p.   cm.
Summary: An illustrated collection of Vietnamese folktales with explanatory notes following each story.
1. Tales—Vietnam.   [1. Folklore—Vietnam.]   I. Hyman, Trina Schart, ill.   II. Title.
PZ8.1.G1668Ch   2001
398.2'09597—dc21   00-8300
ISBN 0-15-224200-7

First edition
A C E G H F D B

Printed in Singapore

The illustrations in this book were done in India ink and acrylic paint on Crescent illustration board.
The display type was set in Eva Antiqua.
The text type was set in Throhand Ink.
Color separations by Bright Arts, Ltd., Hong Kong
Printed and bound by Tien Wah Press, Singapore
This book was printed on totally chlorine-free Nymolla Matte Art paper.
Production supervision by Sandra Grebenar and Ginger Boyer
Designed by Linda Lockowitz

ACKNOWLEDGMENTS

My deepest thanks go to Khanh Vo, who answered a million and one questions about his beautiful homeland; to Van Anh Pham, who helped me translate "The Raven and the Star Fruit"; to Dinh D. Vu, Sylvia, and Daniel for opening their hearts and home to me; to the Tran family for allowing me to be part of their lives; and to Hung, my Number One "son."

In loving memory of
Desla Camp Allison
—S. G.

For Jean
—T. S. H.

CONTENTS

Introduction

To most Americans, the word *Vietnam* brings to mind one thing—a war fought in muddy rice fields and steamy jungles, as we've seen it depicted in movies and popular television programs. Very few of us know much about the history, culture, or folklore of this ancient country.

For ten years after the war ended in Vietnam, the country remained isolated from most of the Western world by its Communist government. But around 1986 Vietnam lifted its "bamboo curtain" to reveal a nation in the clutches of poverty and desperately starving for trade and tourism. The government launched a campaign to attract American dollars and to welcome visitors with open arms. Since 1986 the flow of westerners has steadily increased, and large hotels have been constructed. Reestablishment of diplomatic and economic relations between the United States and Vietnam began in 1994. Today's tourists and businessmen are exposed to a side of the country that was not seen during the war.

As more Americans visit Vietnam they are beginning to see it not as just a place where a tragic war was fought but as a beautiful country with an ancient history and unique culture rich in poetry, art, festivals, and folklore.

The land itself is rugged and breathtaking. Mountains cover three-fourths of the country, and more than two hundred rivers cascade through its jungles and valleys. Though several large cities exist, most Vietnamese live in small farming villages in the flat river deltas (Mekong River in the south and Red River in the north), where rice farming rules their way of life.

The climate of Vietnam is hot most of the year, except in the far north, which enjoys mild winters. Summer is the rainy season, punctuated by strong monsoon winds and torrential showers that often flood the deltas.

Vietnam's location on the eastern side of the Indochinese Peninsula, next to the South China Sea, has exposed the small country to the influences of China to the north, India to the west, and European explorers from the far northwest searching for spices. But the Vietnamese have fought fiercely for hundreds of years to retain their independence and culture.

According to legend, Vietnam's history began four thousand years ago when a dragon prince named Lac Long Quan married a fairy princess named Au Co. They had one hundred children, but this was too much for them to handle, so the parents agreed to separate. Au Co moved to the mountains with half of the children, and Lac Long Quan moved to the lowlands near the sea with the other fifty. Their oldest son founded the first Vietnamese kingdom.

Because of this legendary heritage, the dragon has always been special to the Vietnamese. They consider it to be the luckiest and wisest of all mythological creatures. The emperors sat on dragon-embellished thrones and wore robes embroidered with dragons. In poetry and literature, the Vietnamese call themselves the "children of the dragon."

Vietnamese historians show that the country's first inhabitants were Stone Age clans in northern Vietnam. Their descendants eventually developed a highly complex and sophisticated society with skilled craftsmen and artists. They called their kingdom Au Lac; ruins of their ancient citadel can be seen today near Hanoi.

Eventually the Viets, a group of Asians from southernmost China, migrated over the mountains. They intermarried with many of the people of Au Lac, forming the ethnic Vietnamese race. The kingdom spread over the northern region and became known as Nam-Viet, which means "southern Viets." Eventually the emperors changed the name to Viet-Nam.

In 111 B.C. China invaded Vietnam and ruled for almost one thousand years. The conquerors introduced many customs and three new philosophies: Buddhism, Taoism, and Confucianism. Although China influenced Vietnam greatly, the ancient Viet culture was never completely destroyed. It is still evident in much of Vietnamese folklore.

Some of the country's folktales are actually colorful history lessons about heroes, ancient Viet rulers, and famous battles. Magic, talking animals, and spirits were added as each generation passed the story down to the next.

Other tales teach children lessons in humility, good conduct, and compassion. In these stories the good and wise are rewarded, while the selfish and cruel pay dearly for their faults.

Many of the stories are simple, colorful legends about the origins of plants, animals, customs, or natural phenomena such as the monsoon rains.

Traditionally it is the elderly who tell these stories to children. Although today many of the tales can be found in books as reading lessons, nothing can substitute for the pleasure of hearing the stories—some funny, some scary, and some sad—as Grandmother tells them by the soft glow of the lantern. It is just one more way in which the proud descendants of the dragon prince preserve their culture.

Vietnamese is a tonal language that uses accent marks to indicate its six different tones. The meaning of a word is changed by its tone, just as in English we can change meaning by punctuation marks. For example: *Well? Well! Well…* are all spelled the same but have different meanings. For ease of reading, the diacritical marks have been left off Vietnamese words in this work.

How the Tiger Got Its Stripes

A VERY LONG TIME AGO, when animals could still speak like people, a rice farmer awakened early one morning inside his bamboo hut not far from the jungle-covered mountains. While gray mists swirled over the rice paddies, this farmer led his water buffalo down the dirt trail toward a grazing pasture. Although the water buffalo was many times larger and stronger than the farmer, the slow-moving animal followed obediently. If the buffalo tried to stop to eat some tender young rice plants along the way, the farmer only had to say, "No!" and switch the animal's nose with a small bamboo stick. Never questioning his small master, the water buffalo walked on.

Soon they arrived at a patch of bright green grass on the other side of the clay dikes that surrounded the rice fields. While the buffalo grazed, the farmer settled down under a mango tree to watch the sun rising over the mountains. As he removed his cone-shaped leaf hat, he watched a flock of boisterous ravens fly from tree to tree and listened to the noisy chatter of playful monkeys. Shrill screams of brightly colored parrots filled the air as the farmer began to eat his breakfast of hot tea, and sticky rice pressed between banana leaves.

Meanwhile, in the shadowy jungle, a tiger awakened. He was ravenously hungry because he had not caught anything to eat in two days. His powerful muscles rippled as he stretched his mighty golden body, which back then had no black stripes. As the tiger stalked out into the sunlight on his big padded paws, he spotted the grazing water buffalo. Greedily he watched the large animal, and he licked his lips as he imagined how delicious a buffalo steak would taste.

But when he spied the small farmer, the tiger paused. Though hunger pangs rumbled in his empty stomach, he itched with curiosity.

"Excuse me, Brother Buffalo," the tiger said in his deep growly voice, "but I have watched you come here before. Every day this tiny man leads you here and sits beneath the mango tree while you eat the grass. You are many times bigger and stronger than this little human. Your horns are sharp enough to cut him, and your hooves are hard enough to trample him. The only weapon he carries is a flimsy bamboo switch to slap your face, yet you never stray into the rice paddy or run away."

The dark gray water buffalo slowly lifted his head. Bits of grass clung to his wet nose. He twitched his ears and swatted a bothersome mosquito with his bushy tail.

The tiger sat back on his haunches and lifted a paw as he continued to speak about his observation.

"And in the rainy season the farmer harnesses your shoulders and forces you to pull a plow through the paddies in mud so deep it tickles your stomach. Or he loads your back with heavy bags of rice and drives you to market. I've heard you grunt and moan from the hard work, but still you stay. Why is this, Brother Buffalo?"

The water buffalo swallowed the grass, then he spoke in a smooth, mellow voice.

"I have often pondered this situation myself, Brother Tiger. But I have not been able to solve the puzzle. Perhaps you should ask my master, Mr. Farmer."

The tiger nodded. He turned to the farmer, who was pouring some hot tea into an empty coconut shell. The farmer rose to his feet, a worried expression clouding his face. If the tiger ate his only buffalo, how would he be able to plow his field next spring?

"Please tell me, Mr. Farmer, what makes Brother Buffalo obey you so willingly?" asked the tiger.

"I will tell you, sir," the farmer replied. "I have something that gives me power over all animals. It makes them do the hardest work for me. It is called wisdom."

"Hmmmm...how very amazing," said the tiger. "I would do anything to see this thing you call wisdom. Would you be so kind as to show it to me?"

"Certainly, but it isn't here with me. I keep it inside a gilded box carved with dragons and a golden phoenix. I must go back to my hut to fetch it."

"Good," the tiger said with a sly smile. "I will stay here and watch over the water buffalo for you while you are gone."

"But, sir, how can I let you do that, when you look as if you haven't eaten in a long time? My water buffalo would make a delicious meal for you, I'm afraid."

The tiger smiled his most sincere smile. "I promise not to eat your buffalo while you are away."

The farmer scratched his chin and shook his head. "Now, it isn't that I do not trust you, Mr. Tiger, but I have heard your stomach rumble. How can you resist your hunger with such a mouth-watering temptation in front of you, no matter how honorable your intentions? Why don't you let me tie you up to that coconut palm tree? Then I will be happy to go get the wisdom you want to see."

The tiger was indeed anxious to see the thing called wisdom, so he gladly agreed to be tied to the tree. But he thought, *When the farmer returns and unties me, I will jump on him and rip him apart with my sharp claws and teeth. After that I will eat his water buffalo. With his magic box of wisdom, I shall command cows and deer and delicious wild boars to lie down at my feet. I shall never have to spend my days hunting for dinner again.*

With a bow the tiger strolled up to the palm tree, stood on his hind feet, and held up his front legs.

"Go ahead and tie me up."

The farmer unfurled a rope that he sometimes hooked to the buffalo's nose to lead him about. He wrapped it around and around the tiger's golden body until the hungry beast was secured to the palm tree. Then the farmer left, but he soon returned carrying something behind his back.

The tiger eagerly peered at the small man.

"Did you bring the wisdom for me to see?"

"Yes, I will show you my wisdom. But I don't keep it in a box, foolish tiger. It is here in my head with me all the time. Now I will teach you to stay away from my precious water buffalo."

Quickly the farmer pulled a small burning torch from behind his back and set fire to the weeds at the tiger's big feet.

"Owww!" The tiger howled as the flames began to burn his paws and lick at the rope.

The smell of the tiger's singed fur filled the air as the rope turned black. At last it burned in two and fell to the ground, freeing the tiger. As fast as lightning the tiger fled into the deep, dark jungle.

When the tiger felt safe, he stopped at a pool of refreshing mountain water to drink. He saw his reflection and roared. Big black stripes now circled his golden body. The tiger knew he would never forget the magic called wisdom.

Meanwhile, Brother Buffalo, happy that he was saved from being the tiger's lunch, laughed so hard that he fell and hit his mouth on a rock, knocking out his front teeth.

And this is why the water buffalo has no front teeth and the tiger has stripes.

IN THE PAST, *hundreds of tigers roamed Vietnam, but unfortunately many of them were killed in the last war and others were killed by poachers. Today the beautiful tiger is almost extinct in Vietnam.*

The Vietnamese word for water buffalo is con trau. *A full-grown male can be six feet tall at the shoulders and weigh up to twenty-five hundred pounds.*

Con trau raised in the mountains by tribesmen are aggressive fighters. The males (bulls)

must defend the females (cows) against marauding tigers, wild boars, and other fierce jungle animals. The bulls also often fight one another for the affection of the cows. Bulls charge at each other at a tremendous speed, colliding head on. Then they lock their large horns, and each tries to twist his opponent off balance and break his neck. These mountain water buffalo are often too fierce and temperamental to be good farm workers. Con trau *raised in the flat lowlands, such as the Mekong Delta, where mostly rice is grown, are more obedient and patient.*

Boys and young men usually take care of the con trau, *watching over them to make sure they do not get into the rice fields or wander off. These boys or young men are called* chan trau *or "buffalo boys." They love the* con trau *as much as a family pet and often sing songs to the buffalo to pass the time or to pacify them.* Con trau *love to soak in pools of water, and buffalo boys can sometimes be seen sitting on their backs, fishing.*

Con trau *are very strong and can trudge through thick mud. This is why they are used to plow the rice paddies, which are flooded during rainy season. Ordinary tractors would not work in such wet earth.*

The con trau *were especially invaluable to the Vietnamese during their war against the French. These big animals carried hundreds of pounds of supplies and munitions over muddy roads and fields to the Vietnamese soldiers, where jeeps, trucks, and army tanks could never go.*

The water buffalo, like other members of the bovine family, do not have upper front teeth, but rather, hard gums.

Chu Cuoi—the Man in the Moon

LONG, LONG AGO a poor woodcutter named Chu Cuoi lived in a humble bamboo hut beside the jungle. Every day he carried his ax into the woods to cut small trees and gather dry sticks. Then Chu Cuoi would tie them all into bundles and carry them home on the ends of a long wooden pole that he balanced on his shoulder. Because Chu Cuoi was poor, he could not afford an ox to pull his wood cart to market, so he would walk all the way to town dragging the heavy load himself.

One day while chopping wood in the jungle, he came across three tiger cubs frolicking and wrestling in a clearing. Their mother had left them there while she hunted for food.

If I can catch one of those cubs, Chu Cuoi thought, *I can sell it for a great price and buy an ox.* Quietly he laid down his bundle and crept toward the playful cubs.

He hid behind a fallen log until one of the cubs rolled right up next to him. With a shout he grabbed it by the back of the neck to keep it from biting and scratching. When the other two cubs saw what happened to their brother, they stopped fighting and scampered away, crying and whimpering. Just as Chu Cuoi started to walk away with the squirming tiger cub, he heard a great roar. He turned around and saw the mother tiger, who had just dropped a limp deer at her feet.

With a scream Chu Cuoi scrambled up a tree with the tiger cub in his hands. But the cub wriggled out of his grasp and landed very hard on the ground below. Chu Cuoi watched the mother tiger trot to an old, twisted banyan tree growing near a bubbling stream. She tore some of the leaves off the tree and chewed them up. Then she returned to the motionless cub and placed the chewed leaves on his head.

With an angry growl, the baby tiger leaped to his feet and began chasing the tail of his nearest brother as if nothing had happened. The mother licked the cub, then led her family to the deer, and they began to eat.

After the family of tigers left, Chu Cuoi climbed down from the tree and walked to the bubbling stream. He plucked a few leaves from the ancient banyan tree and sniffed them.

"They smell the same as any other banyan leaves," he said aloud. "Maybe the tiger cub was only stunned. Perhaps he would have gotten up anyway. But just in case, I'll put some of these leaves in my pocket and study them closer when I get home." Chu Cuoi gathered up his ax and started back.

As Chu Cuoi tread down the dusty road that led to his hut, he saw a small dead dog lying in a ditch. He knew that the dog belonged to the son of another woodcutter and that the boy would be brokenhearted. Remembering what he had seen the mother tiger do, Chu Cuoi chewed some of the banyan leaves that he carried in his pocket. He placed the mixture on the head of the dog. With a yelp the dog bounced to its feet, licked Chu Cuoi's hand, then ran down the path as good as new.

"It is an enchanted tree, indeed," Chu Cuoi cried out, and as fast as his feet would carry him, he ran home and got some digging tools. He returned to the stream in the jungle and uprooted the banyan tree and brought it home. He dug a hole deep and wide for the tree, even though it meant destroying his melon patch and cabbages to make room for it. Chu Cuoi took great care with the tree, treating it with respect and kindness. It flourished and grew stronger.

A few weeks later, just before Tet, the lunar New Year's celebration, Chu Cuoi set off to town loaded down with bundles of wood, tree branches covered with delicate pink peach blossoms, and some bright yellow *hoa mai* flowers. He hoped to sell a lot of wood in the marketplace, because everyone would be cooking lavish meals for the long festival.

He waved to women who were on their knees, carefully pulling weeds and clearing away dirt from the tombs of their ancestors to make way for the spirits that always returned to Earth during Tet. Chu Cuoi nodded to friends he hadn't seen for a long time, as they returned to the village of their birth.

Chu Cuoi loved this time of year, not just because he sold a lot of wood but because people were always joyful. As he came to the town, he expected to see villagers dressed in their finest clothes and jewelry. He expected to see children playing games and singing songs with their visiting cousins. But as he walked down the silent street, he saw many sad faces. He stopped beside an old man with a white beard who was decorating his front door with red good-luck banners.

"Excuse me, Honorable Uncle, but why is everyone so sad during this season of joy?"

The frail old man removed his small black hat and wiped his brow before pointing toward the east.

"As you may know," he said, "over that mountain lives the great lord who owns

most of the land in this region. He has a beautiful and gentle daughter, Nguyet Tien, whose favorite pastime is planting lovely flowers over the land."

"Yes, I have seen her from afar. I have heard of her great beauty and gentle nature. But why is everyone sad?" Chu Cuoi asked again.

"Because this lovely girl now lies on her bed, so ill that she is not expected to live through Tet. Although her father owns land as far as the eye can see, and gold and precious gems, all the riches in the world cannot make her well. Every day she slips deeper and deeper into a dark, endless sleep."

When Chu Cuoi heard the awful news, he was greatly disturbed. What a terrible loss if the lord's daughter should die.

Ever since Chu Cuoi had found the magic banyan tree, he carried a few leaves in his pocket in case he came across a wounded animal or a sick friend. Also, he found that the leaves cured the little cuts and bruises that woodcutters so often get while chopping wood.

So Chu Cuoi laid down his bundles of sticks and flowers and set out for the great lord's palace. He walked all day and finally arrived very tired and covered with dust. He was such a sight in his bare feet and ragged clothes that the guards at the palace gates refused to let him in. Over and over he tried to convince them that he could cure the lord's daughter.

"Be gone, beggar!" a guard said, shoving him so hard that Chu Cuoi tumbled down the steps and cut his foot. Chu Cuoi removed a small banyan leaf, chewed it, then placed it on his foot. Instantly the bleeding stopped and the wound healed over. A moment later his foot looked as if it had never been cut.

The surprised guards looked at each other, then quickly helped Chu Cuoi to his feet and led him into the chamber of the lord's daughter. Chu Cuoi took a deep breath when he saw how beautiful Nguyet Tien was. But her face was very pale and she hardly breathed.

Chu Cuoi took the rest of the banyan leaves from his pocket, and breaking them into small pieces, he placed them gently on the girl's tongue. In a moment the color began to return to her cheeks. She opened her eyes and smiled at her father, who stood nearby.

Her father threw his arms around Chu Cuoi, weeping for joy. "Woodcutter, you have saved my daughter's life. For your good deed I grant you her hand in marriage and some of my richest lands."

The lord instructed his men to give Chu Cuoi a bag of gold so he could build a proper house for his new bride.

Chu Cuoi built a lovely house in the same spot where his bamboo hut had stood, being very careful not to disturb the magic banyan tree. By now its twisted roots had sunk deep into the soil of his courtyard.

When the house was ready Chu Cuoi brought his new bride to live with him. As soon as Nguyet Tien settled in she began planting her favorite flowers. She planted pink and white peony bushes and sweet orchid vines. She planted lotuses in the fishpond and jasmine around the walls. And fragrant ginger, too.

Chu Cuoi loved his new wife dearly and allowed her to plant flowers everywhere, with one exception.

"You must never plant flowers around this banyan tree," he told her the first day she arrived. "You must never, never disturb its roots or something terrible might happen. But the rest of the grounds are free for you to landscape as you choose."

Nguyet Tien agreed, but after two months the only spot left unplanted was the patch of earth around the banyan tree. "What am I to do?" she said one day as she stood with a handful of fresh tubers that a friend from the south had brought her. "These dahlias are my favorite, but the only place left to plant them is forbidden. Surely my kind husband won't mind if I put them there. I know I can dig very carefully and not disturb the banyan tree's roots."

Although Chu Cuoi now had enough gold to buy anything he needed and had a fancy house, he was still a simple woodcutter at heart. He missed roaming the jungle to gather wood and seeing the animals play. So, often Chu Cuoi walked into the forest just to be alone and enjoy nature and play his bamboo flute.

While Chu Cuoi was strolling in the jungle, Nguyet Tien decided she would plant the new dahlia tubers under the banyan tree. Very carefully she dug into the earth, but suddenly her shovel slipped and cut one of the tree roots in half.

Nguyet Tien jumped back and screamed in fright as the big tree groaned. It swayed from side to side and slowly began pulling its roots up, one after the other, and started climbing into the evening sky, where a full moon was rising.

When Chu Cuoi heard his wife's screams, he came running back to his house. Just as he reached the courtyard, he saw the last root coming out of the soil. With a shout he grabbed the root and tried to pull the tree back down, but the mighty banyan was very strong. Chu Cuoi clung to the root with all his might as the tree climbed higher and higher into the cloudless sky. Far below he saw his weeping wife and courtyard growing smaller and smaller. Then he saw the village, looking like a cluster of dots, as the tree continued to soar upward. It crossed the heavens, passed the stars, and soon came to rest on the moon. There it sank its roots into the soft yellow moondust.

To this day, if you look very hard on a bright moonlit night, you may just be able to make out the figure of Chu Cuoi sitting under his banyan tree with his flute. There he looks down on Earth and wonders how he will get back home.

THE TALE OF Chu Cuoi is a favorite story told on the night of Tet Trung Thu, or the Moon Festival, which occurs in early autumn when the golden harvest moon hangs in the sky. At dusk children light candles inside colorful lanterns made of thin rice paper and bamboo. Being ever so careful not to let the lanterns catch on fire, the children march in a lantern parade, singing songs. Children also fly kites and watch puppet shows.

Afterward, they indulge in special rice desserts called "moon cakes" or eat fried watermelon seeds, accompanied by hot jasmine tea. Outside under the full moon, children then gather around their grandmothers and listen to fairy tales.

Tet, *the lunar New Year's celebration mentioned in this story, is the most important celebration in Vietnam. Occurring between mid-January to mid-February, Tet signifies the arrival of spring. The festival lasts two weeks, with preparations beginning many days before the actual New Year's Day. It is a time of visiting family and friends, giving gifts, eating lavish meals, and clearing up all debts and worries so that the coming year will start out right. Peach blossoms, yellow* hoa mai *blooms, and miniature orange trees are as traditional to Vietnamese as Christmas trees are to Americans. Many people also hang red paper banners with holiday greetings written on them in the ancient Vietnamese* chu nom *characters that closely resemble Chinese writing.*

Banyan trees are members of the fig tree family and grow in many parts of Asia and India. Their roots appear to grow above the ground in a tangled mass, but in reality the tree branches send down runners that attach to the ground and form new trunks. Very old banyan trees have so many roots and branches that they look like a small grove.

The Legend of the Monsoon Rains

DURING THE FIRST DYNASTY of ancient Vietnam, Emperor Hung Vuong had a beautiful daughter, named Mi Nuong. The emperor loved his only daughter more than anything in the world, and when she became old enough to marry, he wanted to choose only the best husband for her.

Princess Mi Nuong was perfect in every way, with the grace of a willow, the sweet voice of a nightingale, and a face as pure and smooth as a lotus blossom. So renowned was her beauty that suitors came from all corners of the land, seeking her father's consent to marry her. Each man brought exotic and rare gifts and proclaimed his riches and power.

The emperor listened to each suitor, then rejected them one by one. Though some were handsome and some were rich and some were wise, none of them had the combination of all traits that would make the perfect match for his beloved daughter.

Mi Nuong was not as choosy as her father, and she grew sadder with each rejection.

"When will I ever marry?" she asked her mother one day.

"You must be patient and obey your father's decision, my child," her mother replied. "You are the daughter of the greatest emperor and must marry a suitable prince. Be patient and trust your father's judgment."

So, Princess Mi Nuong waited, sneaking glimpses of the suitors who visited and admiring the splendor of their gifts. But from the stern expression on the emperor's face, she always knew when he was dissatisfied.

Time passed until nearly all the available gentlemen in the empire had been turned away by the old emperor.

One day, while the princess sat in the courtyard playing her *dan ty ba* and watching delicate pink lotus blooms floating on the pond, she heard the loud gong announcing the arrival of yet another suitor.

"Why should I even bother to look?" she asked her handmaiden. "My father will only reject him like all the others. I am doomed to be single until I am so old that no one will want to marry me. How much better it would have been if I had been born with many flaws. Perhaps then my father would not have been so particular, and I would have been happily married by now."

With a sigh, she walked to the stone wall and stood on a bench where she could just peek over the top. She gasped at what she saw at the front gate. For below was not just one suitor but two. Each young lord was as handsome as the other. Each rode in a lavishly decorated palanquin carried by servants in brocaded silk uniforms.

As fast as she could, the princess dashed to her father's golden throne, where he awaited the two guests.

"Oh, please, please, dear, honored father. Choose one of these suitors. They are so wonderful to gaze upon." She sat at her father's knee, her head humbly bowed in respect.

The emperor smiled and gently patted his daughter's hand.

"We shall see, sweet child," he said softly. Then he commanded his servants to admit the suitors.

The two men walked into the grand hall at the same time, their luxurious *ao dai* swishing gently and their tall boots clacking on the polished marble floor. They approached the dragon-shaped throne together.

One young man stepped forward and bowed to the emperor. When he spoke, his voice was gentle, quiet, and sincere. The princess felt her heart beat faster as she gazed upon his handsome face.

"I am Son Tinh, Lord of the Mountains. My realm contains the steepest hills and slopes and the darkest jungles, rugged cliffs, cascading waterfalls, and deep rivers. Fierce tigers and mighty elephants and timid deer are at my command. Rare and delicious fruits and fragrant flowers abound at my golden palace gate. All the treasures of the mountains, such as jade, emeralds, and gold, are laid at my feet, if I so desire. Should I be granted your daughter's hand in marriage, she shall sleep upon a bed of jasmine and orchids, and I promise her eternal happiness."

With a gentle bow, he stepped back. Princess Mi Nuong held her breath. How kind this handsome lord was, as well as being rich and powerful. Surely her father would find no fault with him.

Then she watched the next suitor step forward. His stride was bold, and he held his head at a haughty angle. His dark eyes burned into hers until she blushed and covered her face with a delicate silk fan. When this suitor spoke, his voice was loud and firm.

"And I am Thuy Tinh, Lord of the Seas. I rule the underwater realm, which is far more vast than the mountains. Precious pearls and rare coral and treasures lost by sailors at sea are mine. All the creatures in the ocean are my servants. The mighty whale sings at my command, and fierce sharks obey me when I beckon. I can make the winds wail and spin, and I can make the waters crash against the shores and toss ships as if they were sticks in a pond. My home is a palace made of crystal, and it is more beautiful than any human eye has ever seen. All this shall be your daughter's, and she shall sleep inside a mother-of-pearl shell and reign by my side as Queen of the Seas forever."

Then he bowed and stepped back. He stood with his shoulders straight and his dark eyes sparkled with confidence. Though his temperament was firey, Thuy Tinh, too, would make a wonderful match.

Princess Mi Nuong tried to hide her joy. Another perfect suitor. Two in the same day. No matter which lord the emperor chose, she would be lucky indeed. With hope burning in her heart, Mi Nuong turned her eyes to her father, who sat on his throne, stroking his wispy gray beard with his long, curved fingernails.

"Hmmm…two princes so fine in every way. It is such a difficult decision. How can I choose?"

The two lordly princes looked at each other but said nothing. They would abide by the decision of the emperor.

Finally the emperor rose to his feet, throwing back his long embroidered robe as he stepped down from the golden dragon throne.

"This is my decree: Whoever arrives at the first ray of sunlight with the engagement gifts shall be granted Princess Mi Nuong's hand in marriage." Then he lifted his shiny royal sword and passed it in the air over the two men's bowed heads.

The princess clasped her hands together for joy while the two suitors rose from their knees and hurried out of the palace.

Son Tinh rushed back to the mountains and ordered his servants to collect precious jewels, exotic birds, rare and fragrant flowers, and delicious fruits.

Thuy Tinh likewise hurried home to his palace under the sea. He commanded his servants to collect baskets of shimmering pearls and colorful coral and to prepare plates of the most delicious seafood dishes ever cooked. But before sleeping in his great mother-of-pearl bed that night, he threw a lavish celebration party, so confident was he that he would win the contest. Late into the night the Lord of the Seas and his subjects drank and sang and danced.

The next morning, Son Tinh, Lord of the Mountains, and one hundred servants traveled up the road to the emperor's palace while the sun was just beginning to peek over the eastern horizon. He laid the engagement gifts at the emperor's feet.

The emperor was greatly pleased and handed him Princess Mi Nuong. They exchanged wedding vows in a sacred ceremony.

"My daughter is yours now," the emperor said. "Honor and love her as I have.

And daughter, obey your husband as you have obeyed me. I wish you great happiness and many children."

Son Tinh thanked the emperor, then helped the princess into his richly carved palanquin. As the couple started to leave, they saw a long procession coming in their direction. Soon they recognized Thuy Tinh, Lord of the Seas, with his entourage of sleepy, red-eyed servants carrying many precious gifts.

"You are too late, my brother," called out Son Tinh. "Mi Nuong is my bride now."

Thuy Tinh's face burned red with anger as he cried out, "You used trickery! You came before the sun rose." Then with a loud shout, he drew his sword and commanded his men to seize the princess.

Son Tinh drew his sword, too, and shouted to the mountains, "Tigers, leopards, elephants, monkeys, pythons—all beasts of the mountains—I command you to be my soldiers. Come and fight with me against this madman!"

Not to be outdone, Thuy Tinh shouted to the ocean, "I command the creatures that crawl on the bottom of the sea and that swim in the midst of the waters, both great and small, to become my warriors and fight this thief who stole my princess."

Soon a terrible battle began. With a wave of Thuy Tinh's hand, the winds began to howl, bending the trees to the ground. The ocean waves crashed against the rocky shore and rose higher and higher. Day and night the rains slashed through the sky and pounded the earth. Soon huts washed away, rice fields flooded, and the villagers fled for their lives.

As Mi Nuong and her new husband climbed up the mountains, Son Tinh hurled down lightning bolts at the pursuing Lord of the Seas. He pulled up trees and rolled them down the mountainsides, but still Thuy Tinh and his watery army came after them. Every river they passed overflowed its banks and drowned innocent villagers. All over the land, humans and animals scrambled for safety.

The battle raged for weeks between the powerful lords, with neither gaining victory. The villagers knelt before the altars of their ancestors and prayed that the lords would soon tire of the war.

Finally, Son Tinh used all his magical powers to make his favorite mountain grow very high, higher than anything else on Earth. Thuy Tinh saw that he could not make his waters reach the top, so he retreated down the mountains and back to the sea. The rains stopped, the winds calmed, and the waves receded as he sadly returned to his ocean palace.

The villagers returned to their huts and began to work very hard to plant rice in the flooded paddies. They found that the seedlings grew fast and straight and strong from all the rich soil washed up from out of the riverbeds and down from the mountainsides.

But the haughty young lord, Thuy Tinh, has never accepted defeat nor given up trying to win back Princess Mi Nuong. Every year—around June—he returns, and the battle renews. Again the rains fall fast and heavy, the winds bend the trees to the ground, and the waves crash against the shores. Thuy Tinh is determined to steal Mi Nuong, but every year he cannot win and eventually retreats back to the sea.

It is a never ending cycle; and that is why the monsoon rains come to Vietnam every year.

VIETNAM IS LOCATED *in "monsoon Asia." Every year, beginning around June, steady winds blow from the southwest. These winds, which are called monsoons, travel over vast bodies of*

water, such as the Indian Ocean, before reaching Southeast Asia. When the moist winds approach land, the rain begins to fall. The first rains are very heavy and often cause flooding. This rainy season continues all summer until around November.

In the autumn the monsoon winds change directions. Now they blow from the northeast, and since they travel over landmasses, they do not carry as much water. This is called the dry season, and often the land becomes parched. Certain regions of the central highlands, which do not receive as much water as others, are so dry that cacti grow there.

During the seasons when the monsoon winds are switching directions, the weather can be very violent along Vietnam's coastline where it meets the South China Sea, particularly in the central area near the old imperial city of Hue. Destructive storms called typhoons hit the town, sometimes demolishing buildings and flooding homes.

But despite the destructive nature of the monsoon rains, the farmers of Vietnam depend on them to grow rice, the nation's main food crop. Rice seeds are planted in flooded seed beds. Tiny green seedlings are pulled up, tied into bundles, and carried to the large rice fields where they are transplanted in straight rows. All this is painstakingly done by hand, and during planting season there is little rest for the hardworking farm families. The success of these rice crops depends on the arrival of the monsoon rains.

Although these rains may seem inconvenient, the Vietnamese have learned to live with sudden showers, flooded streets, and strong winds. From cone-shaped leaf hats called non-la that shed water, to houses built high aboveground on stilts, to a complicated system of irrigation canals and dikes, the Vietnamese have adapted well to the annual battle between the Lord of the Mountains and the Lord of the Sea.

The Boatman's Flute

ONCE, IN THE Land of Small Dragon, a wealthy mandarin lived in a large mansion on top of a hill overlooking a peaceful river. The mandarin had only one daughter, and her face was as beautiful as lotus blossoms in pale moonlight that floated atop the river.

The mandarin loved his daughter dearly and feared for her safety so much that all her life he had never allowed her to leave the mansion. She spent her days and nights in her room, high above the river, watching the world below. Servants brought her the most delicious dishes, and talented seamstresses sewed her the finest gowns of silk. Musicians and poets sang to her the ballads of old.

But never had the beautiful girl walked barefoot on the dewy green grass nor plucked ripe fruit from a tree nor run along the banks of the river, flying kites and laughing like other children. The only sunlight that ever touched her fair skin was the few pale beams that peeked through the dappled shade in the walled-in courtyard.

One day the mandarin's daughter sat beside her window looking at the small boats and sampans gliding over the peaceful blue waters below. Some were loaded with fresh fruit from the mountains, others with bags of rice or baskets of fish, and some ferried passengers back and forth across the river.

As she watched the activity below, one small *ghe* caught her eye. The boatman stood up and skillfully steered the *ghe* out into deeper water with a long bamboo pole, then he sat down. He placed a bamboo flute to his lips and soon the most haunting, beautiful melody the girl had ever heard drifted up to her window. It was the sound of rippling waters and cool breezes, of tall bamboo and the night bird's song, all woven together. She watched the boatman, and as she listened to the sweet notes rise and fall, she imagined how young, strong, and handsome he must be.

All that day the mandarin's daughter stayed beside the window, until the sun began to set over the western mountain and the boatman steered his *ghe* away out of sight.

That night she dreamed of the strange melody and imagined herself stepping into the boat beside the young man, whose strong arms lifted her aboard with grace and ease. In her dream they drifted along the peaceful river by the light of a full moon. The boatman explained to her all the strange and wonderful sights that unfolded before them. She experienced things that she had only heard about from the poets—the sweet touch of the cool river waters on her hands trailing beside the boat, the gentle kiss of the night wind against her flushed cheeks, and the tingling fragrance of wild orchids hanging from trees in the nearby jungle.

A smile flickered across her lips, even as she slept. She dreamed of climbing out of the boat and running barefoot through the thick green grass and plucking wild berries that burst with a sour, tangy taste on her tongue. And when a green-eyed tiger roared deep in the jungle, the boatman held her tight.

The girl awakened to the sound of a brass gong. Without even stopping to taste the tray of delicacies laid out before her by her devoted handmaiden, the mandarin's

daughter walked to the window and looked below. Her heart beat faster when she spotted the little boat and heard the haunting music floating up to the window once again.

All day she remained by the window, until she knew the tunes he played by heart. Whenever the boat came close to the foot of the hill, she dropped flower petals, hoping the wind would carry them to the boatman. If ever he looked in her direction, she waved her long silk scarf. She became convinced that he played the tunes just for her.

Every day the mandarin's daughter listened to the boatman's melodies, often making up her own words to sing along. Or she danced with her shadow, pretending it was the strong, young boatman. Every night she dreamed of riding down the peaceful

31

river by his side. She knew that her father was planning for her to marry soon and prayed that somehow the boatman was really a lord in disguise who would be the one her father chose.

As for the boatman, he had seen a tiny figure at the window and had caught the petals floating down from above. He could only guess what the girl might look like or who she might be, but just knowing that she was listening made him pour his heart and soul into the melodies.

One day a gentleman he was ferrying across the river noticed the fine quality of the music. "Boatman, for whom do you play your little bamboo flute with such love and feeling? I see no maidens nearby."

The boatman smiled timidly and looked upward. "I do not know her name, but she comes to the window in that house high above the river every day and often drops flowers to show her approval."

The gentleman looked up toward the window, then laughed aloud. "You are a fool, young boatman. That is the mandarin's daughter—the most beautiful girl in all our land and one who is sought after by the most wealthy and powerful men, including myself. How could you be so foolish to think she would ever love a common, plain boatman like yourself?"

The boatman said nothing but sadly put away his flute and steered the boat down the river, for it was growing dark. *Better that I should leave now, while she is but a vision in my mind,* he told himself. *If ever I see her face, I will never have peace again.*

So it was that the boatman decided not to go to that part of the river anymore.

The next morning, when she went to the window, the mandarin's daughter did not see the small *ghe*. She thought of ten thousand excuses why the boatman might be late. As the day wore on, he still did not come. The girl's heart grew heavy and tears dropped

32

from her dark, sad eyes. She refused to lie on her bed that night but instead knelt beside the window, staring at the dark river below.

Another day passed and the boatman did not come, and by nightfall the girl was weak from hunger and weeping. She soon fell ill. The servants placed her on her bed and summoned her father. The mandarin called in the best physicians, but they could find nothing wrong with her. As another day passed, the mandarin grew distraught.

Seeing the mandarin weep over his daughter, the girl's handmaiden could not hold her tongue another moment. She told the mandarin about the boatman who played tunes on his flute that seemed to make the girl very happy. The mandarin ordered his servants to search the river for a man in a small *ghe* playing a bamboo flute.

Soon the men returned with the boatman and his flute. He trembled before the wealthy mandarin, wondering what crime he had committed.

"Are you the young man who has been passing under my window playing tunes upon your flute for many days past?" the mandarin demanded.

"Yes, but I meant no harm. If I have broken a law, it was in complete ignorance. I only played the tunes to pass the long day and because it seemed to please the girl in the window. If I disturbed your household, I beg forgiveness and promise to never bother you again."

"It is no bother," the mandarin replied, as he studied the sincere young boatman. "It seems that your simple music has charmed my daughter. Now she is deathly ill, and I pray that your tunes will restore her spirit. I have been searching the lands for the finest husband for my daughter, but if fate has something else in store, who am I to question? Play your flute again, and if my daughter chooses you above all others, then so be it."

The boatman stood amazed. Never in his wildest dreams had he imagined that he might become the husband of this girl so rare in beauty that no man had ever been allowed to gaze upon her face. With a surge of hope in his heart, he raised the flute to his lips with trembling fingers, and he began to play his favorite melody. Soon the tender, warm notes filled the empty halls of the grand house and reached the bed where the girl lay. In a moment she opened her eyes and a smile touched her lips.

"He has returned," she whispered, and she begged the handmaiden to help her to her feet. With renewed energy, the girl walked through the house to the source of the music. At first her heart pounded as she saw the strong, young man from afar. But as she came nearer and saw his face, her eyes grew cold. Though his body was young and strong, the boatman's face was ugly. Out of politeness, she gave a slight bow.

"Thank you for playing the lovely music on your flute. I feel much better now. Father, please pay the boatman for his kindness and do not worry about me. I am over my illness." Quickly she returned to her room and once again looked out the window at the boats coming and going on the river below, wondering how she could have been so foolish to dream about a simple boatman.

But the boatman's heart was torn apart. He had gazed on a face that men see only in their dreams. He refused to take the bag of gold the mandarin offered, and left the mansion with heavy footsteps. No longer did he have the desire to play his flute, for the music reminded him of the beautiful girl. Neither did he have the spirit to work on the peaceful river, for it, too, reminded him of the girl. Everything he saw or did caused his heart to ache with great longing for the girl that he knew could never love him. Finally, many months later, he lay down and died of a broken heart.

When friends and relatives prepared to send the boatman's body down the river in a farewell voyage, they saw that it was gone. But in its place, where his heart would have been, lay an exquisite piece of green jade. A relative took the jade to a carver, who shaped it into a beautiful drinking goblet.

Sometime later the relative sold the goblet to the mandarin, who gave it to his daughter. That night the girl's handmaiden served her cool water in the new gift. As the girl lifted the jade goblet to her lips she thought she heard a melancholy tune that she had not heard for a very long time—something that was both sad and lovely. Then, as she sipped the water, she saw in the bottom of the cup the image of a small *ghe* and the young boatman steering it down the peaceful river.

Suddenly the girl remembered the boatman's sweet music. She thought about all the happy hours she had spent listening to his flute and the wonderful dreams she had dreamed because of him. Since he had left, no one, not even the most handsome suitors in the land, had made her feel such warmth and happiness. Now, it seemed her days and nights were even longer and more empty than before.

Her heart ached with remorse, and tears filled her eyes.

"Dear boatman, your love was the truest I have ever known. You were good and kind, and I made a terrible mistake. Wherever you are, please forgive me," she whispered. A single teardrop slid down the girl's petal-smooth cheek into the goblet. When the tear touched the water, the goblet burst into pieces and a breeze suddenly rushed in through the window. The girl saw a thin wisp of fog rise from the shattered goblet and sail out into the night. The sound of a flute blended with the sound of the night bird's song, but this time the tune was full of joy. The boatman's soul was free at last to go in peace.

SINCE VIETNAM HAS *very few paved highways and few roads, railroads, or heavy trucks, rivers and canals serve as the main means of transporting products. The* ghe *is a small craft seen on*

nearly all of Vietnam's waterways. The boat owner usually stands and guides the boat by means of a long pole. Some of the ghe have straw mat roofs at one end, under which the owners sleep or take refuge from the hot sun. Sampans (tam ban in Vietnamese) are larger boats, usually with sails, that are able to travel along the seacoast.

The mandarin system of government was introduced to Vietnam by the Chinese. Mandarins were highly educated men who held government positions by passing extremely difficult exams. They were the most respected men in their towns.

Not only mandarins but all fathers in old Vietnam chose mates for their children. Sometimes the arrangement was made while the children were still babies, and it was not uncommon for the husband and wife to see each other for the first time at their wedding ceremony. This custom is still practiced in the more rural villages of Vietnam. Even those young couples who meet, fall in love, and choose to marry are expected to obtain the consent of the girl's father and hold formal engagement and wedding ceremonies.

The Raven and the Star Fruit

ONCE UPON A TIME in old Vietnam, two brothers inherited a farm from their father. Hieu, the oldest, was large and strong but lacked ambition, while De, the youngest, was small, intelligent, and kind.

Hieu did the heavy work, like plowing the muddy rice paddies with the help of a water buffalo. He stooped for days, transplanting the small green seedlings to the flooded fields. Every day he pulled weeds and carried buckets of water from the irrigation canal to the paddies to keep the ground wet for the thirsty rice. At harvest time he cut sheaves and threshed the grain.

De loved animals, so he tended the chickens and ducks and fed the water buffalo and took care of the house.

Being the oldest, Hieu married first. A year later De married a pleasant young girl from the village, and according to custom, they lived with Hieu and his wife.

Hieu was glad to have his younger brother to help him with the farm work, but Hieu's wife was the miserly type. All she cared about was money and possessions. She hid Hieu's inherited gold and valuables in a large chest in her room, never once offering anything to her brother-in-law and his new bride, or to anyone else who needed help. She grumbled and complained night and day and was jealous of De's lovely bride. Although Hieu was large and strong, he was afraid of his wife's sharp tongue and so he tried not to argue with her.

One day, after counting her money, Hieu's wife confronted her husband in an angry voice.

"Why do you let De and his wife live here? We hardly have enough room for ourselves. You are the oldest son and the house belongs to you. It is too crowded here now."

"But he is my brother, and he helps with the farm work," Hieu protested.

"Ha! He's so small, he doesn't do half the work you do. Why don't you send De and his bride to live on that little piece of land your father owned near the mountains. It has a house on it."

She complained so much and made Hieu's life so miserable that he finally agreed to send De and his wife to their father's land many miles away. When the young couple saw the small, rundown hut, they wanted to weep. The palm-thatch roof had blown away, and the woven-straw walls had caved in. The bamboo stilts that raised it off the ground had rotted in two.

"What shall we do?" asked De's wife. "The ground is too hard and hilly to plant rice, and you have no tools or water buffalo. There is no pond for raising ducks or stream for catching fish." A tear fell from her eye as she looked at the miserable little hut.

"Don't fret, dear one. I see something of value over here." De pointed to a small tree with a skinny trunk and neglected, thirsty leaves. From its limbs hung a few strangely shaped greenish yellow fruit. When De plucked one and cut it open, the taste was rare and sweet, and the slice was shaped exactly like a star.

"This *khe* tree will be our salvation. The fruit is worth a lot of money, if we can only keep the tree alive and producing."

So, every day the couple carried water from a faraway well and took loving care of the *khe* tree. They pulled up brambles and weeds from around its trunk and kept away hungry insects.

They gathered the star fruit a few at a time and walked to the nearest village to sell them so they could buy rice and supplies. Together they worked hard and diligently to replace the roof of the hut, and De chopped down bamboo to make a new bed and a table and two chairs.

As time passed, the *khe* tree grew bigger and greener and produced more and more fruit. It was now covered with many juicy star fruit that would be ready to harvest in a few days. De's wife was so excited she could hardly wait. She carefully counted the fruit and calculated how much money they would make. It would be enough for a pig and a chicken and a few farming tools. For the first time in many weeks, their future looked bright.

The next day thunderclouds darkened the mountains and a strong wind stirred. All day the couple watched the sky with wary eyes, and when they climbed into bed that night, neither could sleep for worry about their precious *khe* tree.

Suddenly they heard a noise like a mighty wind outside the window.

"Husband, come quickly!" De's wife shouted. "Our tree, our tree!"

De leaped from the cot, ran to the front yard, then stopped. High in the *khe* sat a huge black raven, as large as a man. In its beak was a fresh star fruit. As the bird flipped the fruit around, seeds fell to the ground. The earth under the tree was already covered with bits of fruit and seeds.

De grabbed a bamboo stick and shook it at the raven, but the big bird kept on eating as if he didn't hear.

"Stop that, you terrible bird! Stop eating our star fruit," De demanded and shook the stick again. But the raven still ignored him.

Finally, De threw the bamboo stick at the bird with all his might and hit the raven smack in the tail. It flew off with a loud *"Caw!"*

De looked at the mess on the ground and the empty spaces on the tree where only that morning there had been luscious fruit. His wife brought out a basket and began picking up the seeds and some partially eaten fruit, hoping to salvage some of it.

"Don't fret," De said as he comforted her. "There is still some fruit left on the tree. We'll harvest tomorrow and buy your little pig. I can wait until later to buy farm tools."

So they retired into the house and took turns watching the tree in case the raven returned. But just before dawn, De could not keep his sleepy eyes open.

Suddenly a loud "*Caw!*" and rustling leaves awakened the couple. They ran to the door only to see the ground once again covered with seeds and the raven perched in the tree.

"Oh no!" De's wife cried as she collapsed to the steps and covered her face with her hands. "We are ruined. That terrible bird is eating all our star fruit, and now we will starve and die alone in this deserted place." As big tears fell down her cheeks, the raven stopped eating and cocked his head sideways. To their surprise the bird began speaking as clearly as any human:

> *"Caw! Caw! Caw!*
> If you let me eat the *khe,*
> I'll pay you back in gold.
> But first you must sew a bag,
> And make it three hands by three."

Then the bird spread its huge wings and flew away. De and his wife looked at each other in disbelief. They thought about it and talked of nothing else all day while they did their chores.

"It cannot be true," said De angrily. "How could a raven give us gold? It's just a trick to get the rest of our fruit. I say we should harvest now before he returns."

"Perhaps you're right, dear husband. But what if he is a fairy in disguise? Let me sew the bag three hands by three, just in case."

De finally agreed and his wife sewed the bag that night. When the sun rose over the mountains, they heard the rush of wind and the loud *"Caw! Caw! Caw!"* and ran to the door.

Outside, the raven was standing under the *khe* tree. Quickly De's wife handed her husband the bag and gently urged him forward.

"Here is the bag," De said, presenting it to the bird, "three hands by three. You have eaten all my fruit, so now show me the gold."

The raven spread its large wings in a welcoming gesture. De hopped onto its back and wrapped his arms around the bird's neck. High, high into the sky they flew, and soon the wind whistled in De's ears and the hut below looked tiny and unimportant.

They flew over the village and fields of waving green rice and over rugged mountains where De saw tumbling waterfalls and a herd of elephants splashing in the water. Onward they flew, over sparkling white beaches spotted with tall coconut palms and over little fishing boats in the bay. Soon they were over the sea, and the wind grew so strong that De clung for his life and closed his eyes. Finally he felt the bird slow down and then descend. He opened one eye and saw an island, as small as an ant, in the middle of the ocean.

The raven landed on the island. There were no trees or plants to speak of, only barren cliffs and one large cave with a nest nearby. The raven yawned and hopped up into the nest.

"I am going to sleep now," said the bird. "Get anything you want from the cave and wake me when your bag is full."

Inside the cave De could not believe his eyes. The walls sparkled with jewels. A chest overflowed with strings of pearls and the floor twinkled with pots of gold. De laughed as he lifted up a necklace of pearls and jade.

"My beautiful wife would like this one," he said, "and here's some gold to build her

a house." He selected the things he thought would please her, not caring about himself. When he had finished collecting what he wanted, De awakened the raven.

"But you haven't filled the bag yet," the raven said, rubbing his sleepy eyes.

"It doesn't matter. I have more than enough riches here to last a lifetime," De said with a grateful smile as he climbed up onto the bird's back.

De's wife greeted her husband with hugs, for she had worried about him. She turned to thank the raven, but it was gone.

De and his wife did not gloat over their fortune. They spent the treasure wisely, a little at a time, buying only what they needed to build a modest rice farm and buy some farm animals. They worked very hard and soon made a successful living as rice farmers. Yet they always gave to the needy and helped their neighbors. And they still took care of the *khe* tree and the little hut near the mountains.

On the anniversary of the death of Hieu's and De's father, it was time for the *gio,* the celebration honoring his memory. De traveled to his brother's house to invite him over for the occasion.

When Hieu's wife saw De coming, she blocked the doorway and told him to go away. "I know you've only come here to borrow money," she said. "But we have nothing to spare. Go beg somewhere else."

"I assure you, sister-in-law, I do not need money. I've only come so that my brother and I may honor our father, as all respectful sons are obliged to do."

"*Hmph!* Your house is too far away and the road too rocky. It would hurt my delicate feet. We will come only if you clear a path from our house to yours and cover it with a thick carpet."

"If you wish," De said with a bow.

"You must also cover the entryway of your house with gold. If you truly respect your father, you must make this a worthy feast." She smiled smugly, thinking she would not have to worry about going to visit them now.

Hieu started to protest her unreasonable request, but he was afraid of his wife's anger.

On the day of the celebration, at sunrise, Hieu and his wife heard a knock at their front door. They were astonished to see an exquisite carpet stretching as far as the eye could see. They followed it all the way to De's new house. When they arrived, they squinted, shading their eyes from the gold-covered entryway sparkling in the morning sun.

As they sat down to a lavish feast set out by scurrying servants, Hieu's wife turned green with envy and she began to complain. "De, you must have become a pirate, or you must have turned to some illegal scheme," she said. "How else could you have obtained such wealth?"

"If you are in trouble with the law," Hieu said, "maybe we shouldn't stay here. The authorities may think I am a pirate, too, since I am your brother."

De and his wife broke into laughter. Then De told Hieu the story of the *khe* tree and the talking raven and the island of treasures.

Hieu's wife envisioned the cave and her eyes lit up with greed. "Why, dearest brother-in-law," she said in her most sincere voice, "we knew you were not a pirate. Now, you and your sweet wife have been taking care of your father's little hut far too long. It's only fair that Hieu and I take over its maintenance now. We feel awful for not sharing your father's inheritance. Why don't you move into our house and take your father's hidden gold? After all, it is partly yours."

But De shook his head. "I will gladly let you have the little hut and the *khe* tree. But I cannot take your house and gold in exchange. We are happy here at our modest farm. We don't need a mansion or any more gold."

The next day, Hieu and his wife eagerly moved into the small hut in the mountains. Hieu's wife sewed not one but two bags, and she made them six hands by six, so they would hold twice the gold.

For days they sat waiting for the raven. When it did not come, Hieu's wife complained that De had lied and tricked them out of their lovely home, which now sat empty.

Then one day they heard a rushing wind and saw the raven flying toward them. Hieu's wife sat down, looking as sad as she could and pretending to cry. The raven listened to her moaning, then cocked his head sideways and spoke:

"If you let me eat the *khe,*
I'll pay you back in gold.
But first you must sew a bag
And make it three hands by three."

Hieu stepped up, the two large bags behind his back. "I already have the bag; take me now."

The raven wanted to eat because he was tired and weak, but Hieu's wife pushed her husband onto the bird's back before it had a chance to rest.

Once again the raven flew over the fields and mountains and sea to the island. Inside the cave, Hieu grabbed everything he saw. Soon the two bags were overflowing with gold. He stuffed his pockets with jewels and draped necklaces around his neck and waist, and he put rows of rings on every finger and toe. He waddled to the raven and grunted as he struggled to climb onto the shiny feathered back.

With a loud *"Caw!"* the raven stumbled forward. He tried to fly high into the sky, but his load was too heavy, so he was able only to skim a few feet over the ocean.

Soon the wind grew stronger and the waves whipped higher, touching the raven's feet and the tips of his wings.

"Caw, caw, caw! Drop some of the gold so I can fly higher," he cried in a shrill voice.

Hieu reluctantly dropped a jade bracelet into the sea.

But still the raven could not fly high enough. The bird cried out again, "If you throw away the gold, you will save your life. If you keep the gold, surely you will die. I told you to make the bag three hands by three."

Hieu grumbled and cursed. He knew his wife would lash him with her tongue and would never let him rest if he did not bring home lots of treasure. He removed necklaces and rings and dropped them into the angry, foamy sea. But still he clung to the two heavy bags of gold.

"Look, there is the shore just ahead!" Hieu screamed. "We're almost home. I know you can make it if you try harder."

"Drop the gold! Drop the gold!" the raven screeched.

"We're almost home! We're almost home!" Hieu shouted, as the waves slapped higher and the wind blew harder.

Suddenly a big wave crashed against the raven. With a scream, Hieu tumbled into the ocean. Still clinging to the bags of gold, he quickly sank to the bottom. The raven felt the weight lift from his back. With a loud *"Caw!"* he flew away, never to return.

Hieu's wife sat in the little hut, waiting for her husband, calculating all the things she would buy with the gold. Day and night she waited until she grew very old, but Hieu never came home again.

Sometimes, late at night, Hieu's ghost wanders along the beaches, lugging two bags of gold on his weary, bony shoulders. When the wind rustles through the palm trees and the waves crash against the shore, his voice can be heard moaning, "We're almost home! We're almost home!"

ANCESTOR WORSHIP *and a respect of deceased relatives is an important part of Vietnamese culture. The typical Vietnamese home has a corner set aside for a family altar with photographs of departed loved ones resting on it. Buddhist families place fruit, flowers, and incense at this altar and use it as a place to pray.*

After a parent dies, the first official commemoration occurs one hundred days following. From then on the ceremony occurs annually on the date of the parent's death. Families often observe the anniversary of the death of grandparents as well.

On the day of the celebration, family members decorate the altar and offer the deceased person's favorite foods. Relatives and friends gather to pay respect, if possible going to a temple or church to pray. Women prepare delicious dishes, and everyone eats and drinks and shares one another's company.

Many Vietnamese believe that the spirits of their ancestors protect their house. Family members take care of the ancestral tombs and keep them cleaned, especially during Tet, the lunar New Year, when spirits are believed to visit Earth.

The khe *fruit mentioned in this folktale is called carambola or tropical star fruit in English. Several times a year,* khe *trees produce fruit, which is a favorite in Asia. Some varieties are sweet, others are tangy, depending on the soil composition. The fruit has five sides, and when sliced, each piece looks like a five-pointed star. The taste and texture of the* khe *is very similar to that of white grapes.*

The Bowmen and the Sisters

ONCE AN OLD WOODCUTTER, his wife, and their twin daughters lived at the foot of a jungle-covered mountain. The old man had worked hard all his life and felt very blessed to have daughters to help him in his old age. The daughters, Thao and Hien, had beautiful faces, but each girl had a hump on her back.

Though twins, the girls were as different as night and day. Thao was sweet natured, loving, and devoted to her parents. Every day she drew water for her mother, tended the vegetable garden, and watched after the small flock of ducks. She helped her mother cook noodles and roll rice paper and clean the bamboo hut. She often walked into the woods to gather mangoes, her father's favorite fruit. She never complained about the hump on her back, saying she expected to marry a young man who would value her for herself, not for her looks.

Hien, on the other hand—although her name meant "kind and generous"—was selfish, vain, and lazy. For no apparent reason the old woodcutter made Hien his favorite, and she was very spoiled. Whenever the sisters went to the pond to catch fish,

Hien sat idly by, under the shade of a banyan tree, while Thao rolled up the legs of her baggy black pants and waded into the muddy water with her net.

"I am much too beautiful to get my clothes wet," Hien would complain, "and my delicate hands will smell bad if I touch those awful fish."

But when the chore was finished, Hien would grumble that her basket was empty, and fearing a scolding from her parents, she would beg her kindhearted sister to share the fish.

Often their parents scolded Thao for things that her lazy sister had done. But being generous, Thao had no ill feelings for Hien.

One day the old woodcutter fell ill and could not go into the forest to cut wood.

He called his two daughters over to his cot, where he lay on top of a straw mat.

Thao gently fanned him with a palm leaf and put a damp cloth across his feverish brow. But Hien turned up her nose at the strong smell of medicinal herbs and roots and did not want to come close to her father.

"I am very tired and weak today, my daughters," the woodcutter said. "Go into the jungle and gather dry twigs and sticks and carry them into the village to trade for food. I have been unable to work for two days now, and we are almost out of rice."

Hien pouted and crossed her arms. "That isn't fair! A beautiful girl like me with such fair skin and delicate hands should not have to do harsh work like gathering wood. And the jungle is full of tigers and snakes. It's too dangerous for a pretty girl."

But Thao spoke up quickly, eager to help her sick father. "I can go alone, dear father. I'm not afraid of the dark woods. Let Hien stay here and take care of you while I am gone."

The old woodcutter agreed, happy to have his favorite daughter remain by his side.

Thao meandered through the woods, carrying a large basket and gathering sticks. A strong wind the night before had strewn many twigs and dead limbs on the jungle floor. Soon Thao was so busy picking them up that she didn't notice how deep she had wandered into the jungle. She hummed a pleasant tune and thought how pleased her father would be to see all the wood she was collecting.

When the basket was so full that not another stick would fit into it, Thao stood up and looked around. She realized that she was in a strange part of the jungle, where the dense trees blocked out the setting sun, and eerie shadows engulfed her.

Then Thao saw the flicker of a fire in a small clearing and heard strange noises.

She crept closer to the light, hiding behind a rambling betel vine as she peered between its heart-shaped leaves. Her eyes grew wide at the sight of a band of mountain tribesmen dressed in colorful striped cloth, carrying bows and arrows and chanting as they danced hand in hand around the bonfire.

The strange ceremony fascinated Thao. "How gracefully they dance," she whispered to herself, "and how beautiful is their colorful clothing." She watched a little while longer before leaving. She hadn't gone very far when she remembered that she had left the basket of wood near the betel vine. Thinking how unhappy her father would be if she returned home empty-handed, she hurried back to retrieve it. Just as Thao reached for the basket, a bowman leaped from the shadows and grabbed her.

As the tribesman led Thao into the clearing, the chanting and dancing stopped. The band of men gathered around her with curious eyes. The leader laughed and spoke with a strange accent. "If you want to be released, you must first entertain us. Now, what kind of talent do you have, little one?" The machete strapped to his waist twinkled in the firelight as he spoke.

Thao searched her mind for something to do. "I know a song or two. Would you like to hear me sing?" she said in a soft voice.

The band of men raised their bows and cheered. "Yes, yes, let us hear the girl sing! We love singing."

Thao began to sing, and soon the bowmen grew quiet and even the birds and insects stopped their chirping. The only sound in the deep jungle was her pure, sweet voice rising and falling through the trees like a whispering wind. When she finished, the leader gently released her arms.

"You have entertained us well, little one," he said with a friendly smile, "and now I will keep my promise. You are free to go."

Thao thanked him and turned to leave, but the other members of the band begged her to stay and sing more songs.

"It is very late, and my parents will be worried about me," Thao said. "But if you wish, I can come again another day to sing for you."

The bowmen cheered.

"Promise to come again tomorrow," the leader said. "And to make sure that you return, I will take something of yours." With these words, he removed the hump from Thao's back and handed it to his friend for safekeeping.

By the time Thao arrived at her father's hut, it was dark. At first her parents scolded her for not being prompt, but when they saw that her hump was gone, they chatted excitedly. Thao told them the story of the dancing bowmen and how she had promised to return to sing again tomorrow.

Quickly her sister, Hien, spoke up. "Dear sister, why should you go back into the jungle? Your hump is gone and mine is still here. Be fair and let me go in your place, then my body will be as beautiful as my face."

Thao was not sure this was such a good idea, for she had promised to return and did not want to break her word. She loved singing for the bowmen and did not want to disappoint them.

But when she protested, her father spoke out in an angry voice, "Thao! Don't be so selfish. Let Hien go in your place and have her hump removed, too. Those dancing savages will never know it isn't you."

So Thao bowed to her father's wishes, and the next evening Hien went into the jungle in her place. Hien wandered around and around until it grew very dark. Finally the moon rose and in the distance she heard the chanting of deep voices and saw the tiny

flicker of a bonfire. She followed the light until she came upon a clearing and peeked around a bush.

"*Ugh!* What ugly savage people they are," she whispered, as she looked at their bronze skin, bows and arrows, and strange striped clothing. Nevertheless, Hien stood up and walked into the clearing. Soon the tribesmen saw her and shouted happily.

"There is the singing girl. Let's bring her over by the fire and hear her sing some more beautiful songs."

So the leader gently steered Hien to the bonfire. The bowmen circled around her, then sat down and waited quietly.

Hien began singing, but she was not gifted with a sweet voice like her sister, Thao. Hien's voice was harsh and full of hatefulness, and she could not carry a tune. After a moment the bowmen began to laugh and make fun of her voice, and they shouted for her to stop.

Hien angrily stomped her foot as she yelled, "What do *you* know about pretty singing? You're only a bunch of savages who are no better than wild animals."

The leader turned Hien around, pointed her in the direction of her home, and told her to go.

But Hien pushed him aside and stood with her arms crossed and her face red with fury. "What about my hump?" she demanded. "You took off my sister's hump."

The leader called over his comrade, who had been carefully guarding Thao's hump.

"Here is the hump you want so badly," the leader said as he quickly put Thao's hump on Hien's back. Then he turned her around again and, pointing his sharp machete at her, commanded her to leave.

With a cry, Hien fled from the jungle, and from that moment on she had the burden of two humps on her back.

THE BOWMEN OF THIS FOLKTALE *are members of one of the many minority tribes who live in the hills and mountains of Vietnam. They are descendants of people driven into the hills by the ethnic Vietnamese who settled Vietnam's rich farming lands and pushed ever southward.*

The Vietnamese once called these tribespeople moi, *which means "savages," because they led a simple life and often used bows, arrows, spears, poison darts, and knives to hunt and fish. Today these people are called* montagnards, *which comes from the French word that means "mountain people."*

There are more than fifty minority groups throughout Vietnam, each with their own language and customs. Many of them still practice a belief called animism. This means they believe that everything—trees, rocks, rivers, animals, even the wind and the rain—has a spirit. The people worship these spirits and look to them for omens to help them make important decisions. A rustling tree, a colorful bird, a snake suddenly slithering through the grass, can have great meaning.

The typical montagnard *lives in a longhouse built on stilts to keep out wild animals. Inside live not only the parents and their children, but also grandparents, aunts, uncles, and cousins—sometimes up to thirty people, representing four generations in a single house.*

Dress varies from tribe to tribe, with specific weaving patterns distinguishing the cloth of each tribe. Many of the members wear turbans on their heads, and men often wear machetes strapped to their waists so they can chop paths through thick vegetation. The women generally wear long, wraparound skirts. While working they carry their babies in cloth pouches tethered to their backs. In many of the tribes, women enjoy positions of power. They are heads of households, and the mother's name is passed down to the children rather than the father's. In some tribes, the women own all the land and houses as well.

57

Over the years, various rulers have forced the men of some tribes to perform hard labor, from working on French plantations to cutting down precious hardwoods to building roads or growing cash crops such as poppies. During the many wars that have raged in Vietnam throughout the twentieth century, montagnards have proved their fighting skills to the French, the Americans, and the North Vietnamese.

The men are skillful hunters and sometimes train animals to work for them. They capture elephants and teach them to haul logs, they train monkeys to climb trees and harvest coconuts and fruit, and they train river otters to catch fish for them.